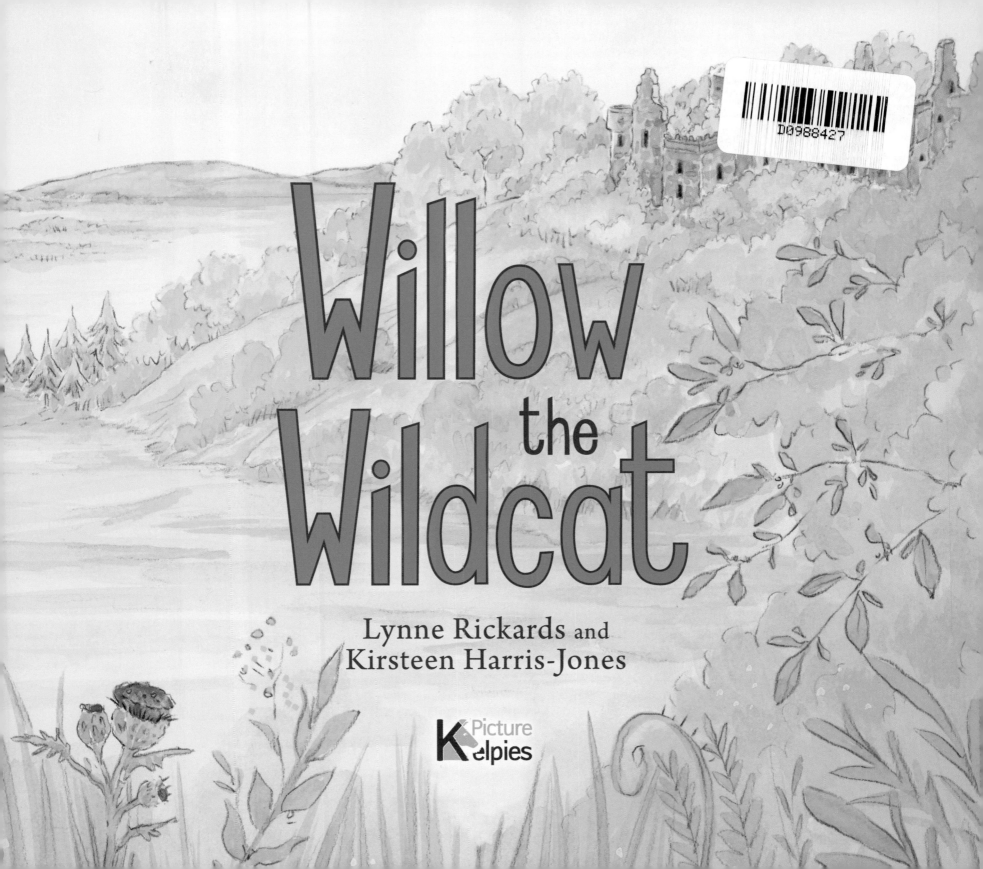

Willow the Wildcat

Lynne Rickards and
Kirsteen Harris-Jones

Picture Kelpies

Two wildcat kittens were wrestling each other.
Willow kept pouncing on Corrie, her brother.

They'd spent all night learning to hunt with their mum,
chased all sorts of creatures, but hadn't caught one.

"You made too much noise," Willow grumbled at first.
"You wouldn't stay still," Corrie growled. "That's worse!"

"It's time to sleep, kittens," Mum called from their den,
but Willow and Corrie were fighting again.

Then suddenly, something was snuffling nearby.
The cats joined their mum in the wink of an eye!

The snuffling came closer – a paw nudged their roof.
The cats curled together, then heard a loud **WOOF!**

Above them, a sheepdog was climbing, and then
it bounded away as the light filled their den.

The logs tumbled down, so their shelter did too.
The three cats were homeless now. What could they do?

They ran to the burn, which was shady and cool.
Mum led the way, till they reached a small pool.

"I'm hungry!" miaowed Willow. "Me too!" Corrie cried.
They'd all missed their dinner, although Mum had tried.

Mum crouched by the water's edge, silent and sly,
watching and waiting for fish to swim by.

"There's one!" cried Corrie, and quick as a flash,
he jumped in and scattered the fish with a **SPLASH!**

"Look what you've done!" Willow hissed at her brother.
"That's ruined our chances of catching another."

Mum said, "Stop fighting! We'll look for a mouse.
And then, very soon we must find a new house."

"There!" whispered Corrie. "A mouse! Let me go."
But Willow pounced first, saying, "You're far too slow."

The mouse saw her coming, and though she was faster,
her mouse-catching skills were a total disaster.

On they all trudged deeper into the wood.
They had to find shelter as soon as they could.

The kittens were tired. They needed to rest.
A tree with some space at the roots would be best.

They came to a spot where the perfect tree stood.
Mum settled the kittens and said, "Now, be good."

"I'll bring you some food. You must stay out of sight.
Sit still and be quiet. Above all, don't fight!"

The kittens felt safe now, inside their new den,
but soon they were back to complaining again.

Willow said, "Move, Corrie – I need more space."
"Ouch!" grumbled Corrie. "Your paw's in my face!"

Then both heard a scrabbling noise overhead.
"Was that in our tree?" Willow whispered with dread.

The scrabbling came closer. It moved down the tree.
The kittens were worried now – what could it be?

A hungry pine marten was sniffing them out,
with bright, beady eyes and a whiskery snout.

Just at that moment, their mum reappeared.
"That pine marten's after my kittens!" she feared.

Mum charged at the tree, and let out a great roar,
and that pine marten **JUMPED** like never before!

The new den was not quite as safe as they'd thought.
It was time to move on again, like it or not.

They came to a field where the grass was so tall
that it gave some protection by hiding them all.

"I can't see a thing!" Corrie said with a frown,
so he climbed up a fencepost to have a look round.

Just then, Willow spotted a giant red kite.
The huge, hungry bird was a terrible sight!

"Watch out, Corrie. Jump!" Willow called from behind ...

He leaped off his perch and escaped just in time!

The red kite swooped down to the fencepost so fast.
Both kittens and Mum bounded off through the grass.

"It's lucky you saw it," cried Corrie in fright.
"Without you, I would have been lunch for that kite!"

"Keep moving now, kittens. Let's hurry!" Mum said.
"It's dangerous here with big birds overhead."

Then suddenly Willow let out a sharp wail.
She was caught on the barbed wire fence by her tail!

"Help me!" she cried. "I can't go any further."
But Mum had gone on – only Corrie had heard her.

He ran back to help her and soon got to work,
yanking her fur from the fence with a jerk.

"Ouch!" exclaimed Willow – but now she was free!
"Thanks so much, Corrie, for rescuing me."

Corrie felt proud, and said, "What do you mean?
There's no way I'd leave you behind – we're a team!"

Soon Willow and Corrie caught up with their mum,
who'd started to worry they might never come!

Together they searched high and low for a gap
in a woodpile, a tree trunk, some place for a nap.

The two wildcat kittens had no time to fight
as they wearily looked for a den that felt right.

This hunt for a home was so hard for the cats.
Then all of a sudden, they stopped in their tracks …

An old ruined castle that kept people out
would be perfect for wildcats to clamber about.

"Look, here!" signalled Willow. She pulled with her teeth to let Mum and Corrie squeeze through underneath.

Corrie helped Willow, then let the fence drop.
Mum was so glad that their fighting had stopped.

She watched as they helped and supported each other,
with teamwork that made her a very proud mother.

Inside, the castle was full of surprises
with so many creatures of all shapes and sizes.

Wood pigeons, squirrels and voles in their nests
would have to make room for the new wildcat guests.

Mum and her kittens explored all around.
What an amazing new place they had found!

Higher and higher they climbed their way through,
till they came to a spot with a wonderful view.

After dinner, the cats settled down for the night.
"This will be perfect," Mum purred with delight.

Willow and Corrie curled up on the stone.
The wandering wildcats had found the right home.